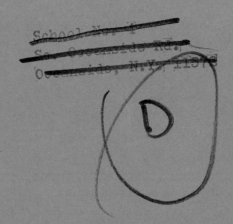

School No. 4
So. Oceanside Rd.,
Oceanside, N.Y. 11572

D

W9-DCX-420

The Little Black Truck

School No. 4
So. Oceanside Rd.
Oceanside, N.Y. 11572

The Little Black Truck

by Libba Moore Gray · illustrated by Elizabeth Sayles

202470T

SIMON & SCHUSTER BOOKS FOR YOUNG READERS

Published by Simon & Schuster

New York London Toronto Sydney Tokyo Singapore

SIMON & SCHUSTER BOOKS FOR YOUNG READERS
Simon & Schuster Building, Rockefeller Center
1230 Avenue of the Americas, New York, New York 10020
Text copyright © 1994 by Libba Moore Gray
Illustrations copyright © 1994 by Elizabeth Sayles
All rights reserved including the right of reproduction
in whole or in part in any form.
SIMON & SCHUSTER BOOKS FOR YOUNG READERS
is a trademark of Simon & Schuster.
Manufactured in the United States of America
10 9 8 7 6 5 4 3 2 1
Library of Congress Cataloging-in-Publication Data
Gray, Libba Moore.
The little black truck / by Libba Moore Gray ;
illustrated by Elizabeth Sayles. p. cm.
Summary: After a hard-working little black truck breaks
down and is towed away, it is repaired and given a second life.
[1. Trucks—Fiction.] I. Sayles, Elizabeth, ill. II. Title.
PZ7.G7793Li 1994 [E]—dc20 92-24413 CIP
ISBN: 0-671-78105-7

For Robert and for Alan
and for The Wellness Community
in Knoxville, Tennessee
—L.M.G.

For Matthew and our
road ahead
—E.S.

The little black truck rolled happily down the bumpy road.

Bumpedy bump
Bumpedy bump
Thumpedy thump
Thumpedy thump

It went past the white-blossomed apple orchard.
It went past the red brick schoolhouse where the children waved as it went rolling along.

It went past the small, brown
grocery store where the owner
gave it a snappy salute.

It rolled on by the sturdy,
steepled church that stood on
the soft green hill.

Beepedy beep
Chug chug
Beepedy beep
Chug chug

It turned onto the road that led
to the yellow farmhouse and into
the whitewashed shed where it
slowed with a

Perka perka
Pop pop
Stop.

The little black truck was a tough little truck. It proudly
carried its load through all kinds of weather, and when rain
or snow came down, the windshield wiper went

> *Squeak squeak*
> *Squish squish*
> *squeak squeak*
> *Swish swish*

and the little black truck just kept rolling along.

In spring it carried baskets of flowers to the sturdy, steepled
church on the soft green hill.

In summer it carried bushels of tomatoes and peas and squash and beans to the small, brown store.

In autumn it carried fat orange pumpkins to the red brick school for the children who waved and hollered when they saw it coming.

In winter it carried bushy green Christmas trees to the yellow farmhouse where one stood in the front parlor covered with glistening glass ornaments and brightly colored lights, and where another stood in the yard decorated with popcorn and cranberries and suet for the squirrels and birds.

Days turned into weeks. Weeks turned into months. And months turned into years.

Spring, summer, autumn and winter, the little black truck hauled and carried.

Beepedy beep
Chug chug
Beepedy beep
Chug chug

The little black truck wasn't shiny anymore. It moved more and more slowly. One day the windshield wiper wouldn't work. Another day the tail pipe fell with a clatter onto the road. One by one, its fine rubber tires went hiss, hiss, hissing, down, down, down. No longer did it go

> *Beepedy beep*
> *Chug chug*
> *Beepedy beep*
> *Chug chug.*

Now it went

> *Chuggedy chug*
> *Chuggedy chug*
> *Sluggedy slug*
> *Sluggedy slug*
> *Shudder shudder*
> *Shimmy shimmy*
> *Slow*
> *Slower*
> *Stop.*

Finally the little black truck couldn't go anymore.

One day when snow came soundless from the sky,
the little black truck was slowly towed away.

It was towed far from the apple orchard, far from the
school, far from the grocery store, far from the church,
and very far from the yellow farmhouse.

In spring, vines crawled over the worn-out frame.
Birds pulled string from the torn seats to build their nests.
Small rabbits nested under the back of the sagging truck.
The little black truck was rust, rust, rusting away.

Dustedy dust
Rust rust
Dustedy dust
Rust rust

Years later, a young man found the abandoned truck.
Thinking it looked like his grandfather's old black truck,
he pulled it out of the woods and down a hill until they
came to a big farmhouse.

The little black truck was put on four cinder blocks.
It was given a new engine, clear windows, soft blue
cushions and four brand-new tires. It was sanded
and painted and polished and buffed until it shone
like black satin.

With its new engine, the little black truck went humming
down the road.

Hummedy hum
Toot toot
Hummedy hum
Toot toot

It went past the golden-leafed apple orchard.
It went past the brand-new schoolhouse.
It went past a shopping center where the small, brown store once stood.
It rolled on by the sturdy, steepled church that still stood on the soft green hill.

The little black truck, loaded with apples and quilts and jars of currant jelly, tooted merrily along. It rolled right through the gates and onto the grounds of the county fair.

At the end of the day when the sun was going down, the little black truck went humming back down the road with ribbons won at the fair — flap, flap, flapping like blue flags in the wind.

Hummedy hum
Toot toot
Hummedy hum
Toot toot

went the little black truck all the way home.